THE CHOIRMASTER
A Bahamian Tragedy

Patrick Rahming

The Choirmaster
Copyright by Patrick A. Rahming

All rights reserved. No part of this book may be reproduced in any form or by any electronic or mechanical means, including information storage and retrieval systems, without permission in writing from the publisher, except for a reviewer, who may quote brief passages in the review. For permission, please send enquiries to
Patrick Rahming
P.O.Box N9926
Nassau, Bahamas

ISBN: 978-0-578-01801-0

*"Man take one an' satisfy
Woman take two an' she make a moo…"*

Bahamian rhyme

CHAPTER ONE

The small brown-and-white mongrel sniffed the pile of rags heaped against the tiled wall, under the endless glass show-window. Pale pink mannequins, with their white-patched skins and mis-matched arms, stared down at him, their painted-on indifference adding to the chill of the December night. Large, old-fashioned Christmas tree lights blinked, their reddish hue pounding the night like a carpenter's hammer. The dog sniffed again, then raised its left hind-leg and relieved itself on the pile, while glancing curiously across the street. In a minute it was aimlessly trotting west on the sidewalk of Bay Street, the main street in the business district of Nassau oblivious to the evidence of commerce generated by the Yuletide season.

A light rain earlier in the evening had caught the early shoppers by surprise. The rainy season for the Bahamas ends with the end of the official Hurricane season at the end of November. During the small downpour, most of the sidewalks had gotten wet, but this spot was protected by the wide, never used balcony above, had remained dry, offering shelter and a kind of tiled warmth. Afterwards the tourists had rushed back to the glitter of their hotels and cruise ships, and many of the natives had retreated over the proverbial hill, into the mist of the densely populated, Afro-colonial settlement called Grants Town. Most, but not all.

As the dog trotted away, stopping occasionally to sniff at other curiosities, the rag pile stirred, and from somewhere within came a man's voice.

"Son-of-a-bitch! Man cyan' lay down, catch a sleep without somebody pissin' on eem?"

An elderly man with an unwashed, unshaven face emerged like some unearthly moth from the offensive pile, and propped himself up against the wall, brushing away the dog's insult. He was the picture of sartorial squalor, three or four pairs of trousers, the top one torn badly at the knee, a dingy grey raincoat over a brown gabardine jacket with no buttons, a formerly-white shirt buttoned to the neck with a number of pens in the pocket, and two different feet of black shoes, both completely worn through. Beneath his derelict walking wardrobe he hid a worn, old, leather briefcase, from which he removed two or three sheets of paper and studied them for a moment, then he returned them to the briefcase, and burst into a baritone solo from the "Holy City". Although obviously in his sixties, his voice was clear and strong, and like an old professional, he seemed determined to keep perfect time. As his volume rose he watched the three tourists approach. Their faces showed that they were uneasy about this vagabond threat to their high priced Christmas cheer. They quickened their pace, and laughed nervously as they hurried away. The old man thought they looked like New Yorkers.

His memories of New York were all winter memories, drawn from his great disappointment in that celebrated American city. In his youth he had dreamed of visiting New York, picturing the glitter and excitement of its gaily-lit streets, its Broadway shows, its wonderful skyscrapers, but when he finally got the chance, it was the pathos and filth that caught his eye: men huddled in partially-heated vestibules, escaping the bitter cold, their bodies covered with yesterday's news; young girls begging for customers in dirty Subway stations, dressed to be killed, wild-eyed young men desperately offering stolen goods in exchange for a few seconds of numbness. He reflected on the fear in the tourist's eyes and decided that Nassau was a damn sight less frightening or pathetic then New York City.

Now, having reached his favourite spot in the aria, he closed his eyes, and remembered himself surrounded by angelic voices-the sopranos floating on a breathless obligatto somewhere above him, held in orbit by the tip-toe tenors, who in turn found themselves bathed in the deep sensuous notes of the altos. Ah! those altos. The old man had been transported to another plane as he performed this piece, backed by the magnificent choir of his memory, here in his own personal, open Cathedral.

The young Policeman's voice shattered his Bay Street recital. The old man, had, of course, not seen the twenty-year-old standing there, a hundred feet away, his personal feelings wrestling with the requirements of his job.

"Choirmaster. Sir. Is Christmas, das true, but dat don't mean you could make noise on Bay Street. C'mon. You gatta go. I don't wan' haveta lock you up. Let's go".

Without stopping his song, the old man collected his belongings and shuffled off in the same direction as the mongrel. A block away, still looking nervously over his shoulder, he crossed the street, in search of a safer spot to continue this concert. Watching him from across the street, two idle taxi-drivers paused in their political discussion.

"Why dis ol' man don't get off Bay Street, with e' stink se'f?"

"Das the Choirmaster. Boy he could sing."

"Wha' kind'a choirmaster? He ain' gat no fambly eh?"

"Boy, lemme tell you. Dat man? Ain' no choirmaster 'roun' here could'a touch him when he was young. He put together one choir fur Caribbean Unification Day one time—mussee 'bout' 400 people --- and I mean dey bus' up one complicated piece 'a music that night. He know what 'e was doin', boy."

"So, wha' hap'n to eem?"

"Woman I hear."

CHAPTER TWO

Those small, slightly-rounded protrusions in the satin robe were her nipples, rising and falling with musical regularity, magnets to the eyes of John Mackenzie, the 50-year old, happily married choirmaster, struggling through the performance of an anthem for which he had suffered endless rehearsals for more than a month. Now, as he approached the difficult transition, a complicated change of pace, his concentration had been all but completely destroyed by those nipples. He closed his eyes to regain his musical balance, and managed to get through the change, and complete the anthem, dripping with sweat. As he collapsed into his special, upholstered chair a few feet behind the Pastor's, he breathed a sigh of relief, un-noticed among the enthusiastic expressions of satisfaction.

"Amen"

"Amen, Bulla Mack, Amen."

The alto-section was as far away as it could be on this platform, yet he could feel the presence of one alto, as if she were bending over him, those nipples hanging like scarlet plums before him, waiting to be mouthed. This service had been the longest, it seemed, he had ever experienced, and the heat of the Church the greatest.

Two weeks ago Sarah Benjamin was just another voice....not an outstanding one, either....which he used on occasion for unimportant solos. Suddenly she was a person with skin and blood and hair, with a certain smell. A real person with arms and legs. And breasts. Two weeks ago his life had been exactly what he wanted it to be, what he had worked to make it for almost thirty years. The mortgage for his four-bedroom, split level house had been paid off, his children well educated, his older two already married, the third a Senior in College, a secure retirement only four years away, and he had recently been elected Treasurer of the Church Board. His family life was nearly perfect. Money was no problem and he had no social complaints. Sarah Benjamin had only asked him for a ride home after a choir practice, and the corrosion began.

"Mr. Mack. I could ask you a question?"
"Yes?"
"Um... How...long you bin married?"

"Oh, 'bout twenty-six years. Best years 'a my life. Why?"
"Well, um...ah...nothin,' ... just curious, that's all,"
"Best years' a my life."

But something about the question disturbed him. She had obviously wanted to say more, but for some reason had decided she should not. Minutes later, he had delivered her to her gate, and was on his way home to Dawn Emily. Suddenly, he found himself reviewing his twenty-six years of marriage, years he had planned carefully and had always been proud of, Sarah Benjamin's question nagged him through the night, and into the following business day. That first telephone call surprised him a lot more that it did her.

"Hello? Miss Benjamin? Dis Bulla Mack, from choir?"
"Yes?"
"I...um, er...I, you...I was wonderin' if you...I... might meet me for lunch sometime. I ... I have somethin' I wan' discuss... thas if you don't mind."

She had treated the lunch as a business appointment, which pleased the nervous Mack. He had been fifteen minutes early, so that he could choose a table out of plain view of the main restaurant, and asked the waitress to keep an eye out for his "business associate". When she walked up to the table, he noticed that this was quite a different Sarah Benjamin from the alto in his choir. This Sarah Benjamin, dressed in a grey-and-white suit, with a coral shoulder bag and high heels, was much more elegant, much more distinctive. Her hair was the same, but the large, gold earrings made the shape of her oval face somehow more sensuous. In fact, it was the first time he noticed that she was really quite attractive. As she sat down, she established that she would pay for her own lunch, and that she had allotted no more than fifty more minutes for this meeting. Mack decided not to waste any of the time.

"Why you ask me 'bout my married life?"
"Me? I ask you 'bout your married life?.....Oh, that, I didn't mean nothing."

As she spoke, she stared into his eyes, reading the seriousness with which he was exploring her 'casual' question. This tall, very black, elegant man reminded her of Sidney Poitier, the film star in a movie she had seen as a young girl. The hair on his temples were nicely white, and the grey in his eyebrows and moustache gave his strong face an air of distinction. She smiled as she remembered telling one of her friends that if she were ever to have an affair in her Church, he would be the first candidate.

"Look, I don't wan' make too much out of it, but you don't ask tha' kind'a question right so. Sup'm make you ask that."
"Well, I don't mean to hurt your feelin's or anything but I find myse'f askin' certain questions bout' you..."
"Like?"
"I bin watchin' you, I bin sitt'n in the choir for ...what...?...three years now?...watchin' you. I useta think "now thas how I wan' my life to be, just

like Bulla Mack. He gat errything. He gat a good married life, good job an' a good position in society. He gat it made'. But the more I watch you, the more I change my mind, cuz I realize…. that ain' me."
"I don't understand?"
"Well… you sure you wan' me talk 'bout this? (Mack nods) OK… It just look to me like, with all you gat… I don't know…you just look bored stiff, I guess."

Mack suddenly felt naked. Naked and transparent. He had never looked at his life in those terms before, and the realization that this young girl could see through his worldly success to the emptiness he had learned to ignore, while taking comfort in everybody else's assurance of his "invaluable contributions" - his wife, his children, his employers, and , of course, the Church, - sent a chill up his spine. Suddenly it was as if this stranger could see him more clearly than anybody else, and the closeness frightened him.

"I'm sorry. I shouldn't have said that. That ain't none'a my business. I'm sorry."
"No, no, no. Thas alright, I don't mind".

Thus began a new kind of relationship in the life of John Mackenzie, one based upon the voyage of discovery through the uncharted waters of his personal satisfaction, and deeper emotional responses, piloted by the unlikely young alto, Sarah Benjamin, a relationship not to be shared with Dawn, Rev or anybody else. He was sure nobody else would understand.

Dawn Mackenzie was reading when Mack got home.

"Night, Honey. Good day?"
"Uh…yeah…yeah. It was OK"
"I called you in the afternoon, but Sherry said you'd been out since lunch-time. I was gonna stop by."

Mack waked quickly into the cedar-lined closet and started to undress in the semi-darkness, stuffing his shirt into the wicker basket. Then grabbed his robe and headed for the bathroom, where he could talk without eye contact. This would be the first lie.

"She didn't know where I was, an' she ain' guh know. I was checkin' up on some stuff outside the office, something to do with the audit. You know?"

She accepted that, of course. In twenty-six years of marriage there had never been any reason to question his word. Dawn Emily, as he sometimes called her, had been his pride and joy when he returned from University, engaged to the most beautiful girl in the Teacher's College, the youngest daughter in a family of seven beauty queens. Her olive complexion and so-called 'good' hair had meant that she had social choice, and few members of her family thought her choice of a husband was appropriate.

When she married Mack, fresh out of school, they had sat down and planned a life together, their planning punctuated by prayers, and the constant rededication of their lives and the lives of their future children to God. Those difficult early years, when they both worked two jobs, lived in small apartments, and caught the jitney to and from work, had taught her that she could always trust him. So without another word, she headed for the Kitchen.

It was Thursday. They would eat pork chops, mashed potatoes and corn, watch television from eight to ten o' clock, discuss the children and the Church for an hour, then fall asleep in their separate, side-by-side beds. She had not noticed that Mack had laid awake until one the night before. Tonight he would not sleep at all.

The first time Mack and Sarah made love was a week later. The choir had been invited to perform at a Church Conference in Freeport, and stayed overnight at a hotel after their performance. Dawn had had some community work to do, and chose not to go, since she could also use the evening to prepare Phillipa's room, who was due to return from University the following day. She would go to the airport to meet both Mack and Phillipa at mid-day on Saturday.

"Bulla Mack. I can't get to sleep."

Mack strained his eyes to read the green fluorescent numbers on the top of the TV controls. It was twelve –forty-seven. AM. Sarah's voice was a soft whisper.

"Dina in this room with me, so I can't talk. I could come up to your room?"

Panic seized his mind. Of course not, he thought. He couldn't do that it wouldn't be right.

"Uh, yeah… I guess. Yeah. But be careful."

Now why did I say that, he wondered? He certainly could not have a woman in his room in the middle of the night. What if Dawn found out? What if anybody found out? Even though nothing would happen, it would be disastrous. Instinctively he reached for the telephone to call her back. The wrong voice answered, and Mack hung up. He quickly got up, got dressed, remade the bed and turned on the TV set. Half hour later she had him in bed.

It was wonderful. He had never seen or felt a body like hers, and the things she did to him he would never have imagined people did. She found ways of exciting him which shocked him. His protests got weaker as his body did, but her devices for rejuvenating his sexual prowess outclassed his protests, and by the end of their second mounting he was completely resigned his carnal enjoyment. On the airplane later that morning, he was surprised by how apparently easily Sarah made small talk with the other ladies, while he was completely distracted by their sudden intimacy.

Dawn asked about the Conference and about the choir's performance Mack told her about the Conference and about the choir's performance.

CHAPTER THREE

"Rev, you ever find yourself questionin' your life? I mean, yuh think yuh life set up just right---you love yuh wife, proud'a yuh children, involve with yuh church --- you ever look down in the congregation an' wonder if some'a them out there ain' get'n more out'a life, with their worldly ways?.... that compared to them, your life ain' just in order----it's just…borin'?"

The Right Reverend Otis Percentie was an officer in the Boy's Brigade when Mack was a Staff-Sergeant. Over the next twenty years, they became the best of friends, through University and early jobs, until they were separated by Rev's transfer to Andros. They had been reunited a year ago, when Reverend Percentie was transferred to Friendliness Baptist Church, where Mack had been the Choirmaster for a number of years. So Mack spoke to him, not as his Pastor, but as his friend.

"Oh yeah. This a time y' know. Them young people thinkin' different from you'n me. They out ta enjoy erry li'l bit' a pleasure they could find. An sometimes I does remind m'sef that this world an' all the wonderful things therein is mine, sayeth the Lord. But then, as a Christian I have a duty to be an example, an' not a stumb'lin' block. The Devil tryin' hard tuh make me forget is the nex' life I worryin' 'bout", not this one. My life might be borin' f' true, but thas the price' a responsibility."

Rev would have been shocked that Mack would drive so far out of his way on the way home, just to pass Sarah Benjamin's house. Or that he would wait outside her computer consultancy firm's headquarters to get a glimpse of her as she left work a few days later. Mack swallowed loudly, fighting the sinking, almost nauseating feeling, as she emerged with a tall, good-looking young man. When they got into Sarah's car, Mack decided to follow, not certain why. From two cars behind, he could see them clearly, and imagined he saw them laughing as they wound their way through the streets of Over-the-Hill, the densely populated, lower-income area of New Providence, where Mack's late-model European car seemed very conspicuous. It was mid-week, and his car was too clean. The ceremony of public car-cleaning and subsequent display was a welcome affair, so the many perfectly-white Japenese and German cars he passed seemed to apologize for their mid-week condition, which made Mack even more self-conscious. Sarah stopped in front of a large yard, filled with wrecked cars, and a few seemingly new ones, all arranged around a large silk-cotton tree. The young man got out, walked over to a shiny, red German sports car, and signaled Sarah to leave. Mack followed to the next corner, then, struggling with his own embarrassment, turned off and went home. As she headed for the Kitchen ,Dawn pointed out to her husband that he was a few minutes late. Again.

It turned out the young man's name was Elvis. Elvis Anthony Bethel. Sarah had introduced him to her sister as "her kind'a man", which meant he was well-educated, made lots of money, and was available for marriage. He was, in fact, the divorced General Manager of an off-shore bank. For whatever reason, Mack had assumed Sarah had no romantic interests, other than him. Elvis was as captivated by Sarah as he was, and in a position to do more about it.

The noise in the adjacent room was almost deafening. It was late in the last quarter, and the score was tied. The crowd at the bar seemed about equally divided in support, and neither group suppressed its vocal encouragement. The excitement of the game seemed to increase with the drinking level, as each basket was celebrated with a ceremony of a deafening roar, the tinkling of glass, and an order for more beer. By comparison, the dining area of the Sugar House was quiet and intimate largely because of the subdued lighting and the high prices.

Mack and Sarah were huddled together, sharing a bowl of conch fritters, both seated on the same side of the table, waiting for their order of chicken souse, when Freda appeared. She slipped into the other seat, slid the bottled candle aside and leaned into Sarah's face.

"What you doin?"

"What you mean?"

"Dis a married man. You just finish get'n hurt by one married man an' you wan' hook up with another one?"

She ignored Mack completely, which made him appropriately uncomfortable. He nervously studied the room's décor - the dark burgundy leatherette chairs, salmon walls, partially covered with prints of local flowers, blackened ceiling with pendulous rattan-bladed ceiling fans lazily churning the candle-lit air, spreading the deliberately loud "soft" music, the stale cigarette smoke, the inexpensive perfume and the smell of fish around the room. He then counted the bodies he could see, and speculated on their similar motives.

"Look, when Freddie walk out leavin' you wit' Carrie ta raise, you come runnin' tuh me, cryin' yuh eye out. One 'a the things you tell me then was you wasn't goin' out with no married man no more."

"Hey, hey! I ain' goin' out with him. He just a friend. You don't have'ta worry, bout that. I allright. I'll be allright."

Sarah's firm response ended the attack. Instead of continuing, the young woman casually turned to Mack, held out her hand, smiled warmly and introduced herself.

"I'm Freda, this child's sister. Sorry 'bout that. Just lookin' out fuh muh big sister. Cyan' blame me fuh that, right?"

Then, with a reproachful glance at her sister she was gone. As Sarah sipped her rum punch, Mack could feel her sly, sideways glance.

"Don't mind Freda. She think she's my ma."
"Who's Freddie?"

Freddie was the Service Manager at Sarah's office, who had wined and dined her, and with whom she had fallen in love. When his wife discovered their affair, she walked out on him. A few days later, Freddie told Sarah he couldn't see her anymore, and left to pursue his wife. For six months she had deliberately kept her relationships shallow, and studiously avoided contact with married men.

"But I don't have'ta worry 'bout you. I won't fall in love with you. This just what I need for a li'l while."
"…a li'l while?"
"Oh, soon as is time you goin' back to yuh safe, borin', life, with everything perfect. An' li'l Sarah here will have'ta move on."

Her tone was teasing, but Mack knew she was serious.

"What you mean, 'everything perfect'?"
"Well, you gat a lovin' wife, three beautiful children an' not a worry in the world. All Sarah is is a ride on a diff'rent kind'a plane, something to make your blood flow. But I ain' no fool, I know you cyan' give up all'a tha' sweetness for this li'l bit….'a sweetness."

She moved her hips closer to his on the bench seat as she spoke, and waited for his reaction. She was not prepared for his embarrassment.

"But…but I thought you liked me."
"'Course I like you. Thas why I here. But I ain' gat no illusions 'bout the future. This is just a temporary thing. Thas all."

They ate the rest of the meal in silence, although Mack felt Sarah's hand on his thigh, stroking him. He felt betrayed. He was risking his marriage, his sanity and his church life for what Sarah was calling a 'temporary thing'. Suddenly he wished he could retract his offer, but the tickets were in his pocket, bought and paid for. He had invited her to join him in Houston, where he would be spending a week at a Convention. This insanity would have to end on his return to Nassau.

CHAPTER FOUR

Mack returned to his hotel room exhausted. His enthusiastic involvement in committee activities at the Convention left him barely enough energy to watch the evening news before falling asleep. On three of the previous nights he had managed a brief call to Dawn, and they had agreed that he would not call again until the final night. As he dropped onto the bed and kicked off his shoes he saw the blinking red light on the telephone. Instinctively, he responded to the universal sign for trouble.

"Mr. Mackenzie? We have a message for you. Please call room 1421."

It was probably another delegate wishing to discuss one of the issues raised before tomorrow's session, he thought.

"Hello?"
"This is John Mackenzie"
"I know Bulla Mack"

Wham! He had completely forgotten that Sarah Benjamin was due to join him that evening. As if she was there watching him, he sat straight up and tried to fix his tie with his free hand.

"You…you…you OK?"
"Yep. You wan' me up there, or you comin' down here?"
"Er… I'll…I'll come down. Gimme ten minutes."

The room was dark, lit only by three slender, black candles arranged strategically around the room, and by the night lights of Houston, the sprawling metropolis, its ultra-modern skyscrapers sparkling and twinkling outside the glazed walls, filtered by the sheer, white inner curtains. Sarah was dressed to match the windows, in a floor-length whisper, her firm silhouette moving effortlessly as she turned to lead him across the room. From somewhere inside the box which housed the TV came soft, romantic piano music, which filled the room with a warm, inviting feeling, a feeling heightened by the faint, sweet smell of burning incense.

She sat him quietly on the bed, then gently pushed him down. As a teenager he had read about Geisha girls, and suddenly he felt he had been transported to Japan, as she slowly removed his clothing, punctuating the ritual undressing with soft singing along with the piano music. Each time Mack tried to speak or raise up, she would gently place her fingers on his lips or chest, and he would surrender again. She poured scented oil onto his body, then stroked, pressed and pulled his tired muscles around, until there was no hint of resistance. He had never felt so completely afloat in a moment's ecstasy, and when Sarah finally handed him a glass of champagne, his hesitation was brief. It was his first drink since College, and as he joined her in a silent toast, he knew he would soon be giddy.

Mack thought of the first time he spoke to this woman.

"'Evenin' Mr. Mack. You gat any space in the choir? I does sing alto, but I can't read music."

She had been innocent, so straight-laced, he thought. Her voice was not exceptional, but he had been impressed by her seriousness. It had been so easy to see her as just another very helpful member of the choir, always present for rehearsals, always willing to run errands or fill in. If he had ever wondered about her life outside the Church, he could never have imagined this.

As she took him from one stage of arousal to another, he protested weakly, wondering how much was humanly possible. Surely he would hurt himself if he allowed this to continue. But somehow he knew she would take care of him.

And she did. In the hours that followed he enjoyed a new role as a student of pleasure. While she led him down paths of unbelievable satisfaction, she tutored and coached him in techniques which offered her both satisfaction and amusement, until, exhausted and euphoric; Mack was magically transported to a strange place, a dreamy fantasy land.

He looked around. He was in a very tall room with long, narrows windows and cool, stone walls. Across the space he could see a long, wooden banquet table, sporting the remains of a feast. On the wall behind hung banners, with images of lions and eagles. This was clearly the days of chivalry, and Mack was one of King Arthur's knights. Beside him, all sharing straw beds, were his friends, whose names he knew to be Sir Lancelot, Sir Gareth and Sir Belvedere. They had apparently singled out four fine wenches to try out the many exotic devices for inflicting pleasure they had brought back from the Crusades. His wench was a most beautiful Moor, bedecked with a gold collar and wonderful wooly hair. Her face was smooth and black, with full lips that sang to him in a voice he recognized. She was Sarah Benjamin. His Sarah Benjamin.

Suddenly the alarm was being sounded. The loud bell filled the room, and Sir Mack jumped up to find himself in room 1421 in a hotel in Houston, listening to the telephone ring. It was the wake-up call Sarah had arranged for him.

As he stumbled up to his own room, bathed and dressed for this last day at the Convention, he could feel Sarah's hands on his body, her legs wrapped around his, her breath in his ear. He would have two nights to enjoy this wench.

But as the taxi wound its way through traffic towards the huge steel-and-glass Convention Center, his thoughts flew back to Dawn. What was he doing? He and Dawn loved each other. She had been his best friend for more than half his life. She trusted him. She had been a perfect mother of his children, having left her teaching career for fifteen years to be at home for them. On this Friday morning, she would have already served Phillipa breakfast, picked up the maid and the gardener, and dropped his suits off to the dry cleaner's. He was once again, aware of the impossibility of this wonderful relationship with Sarah Benjamin.

CHAPTER FIVE

By the next Wednesday night Mack's emotions had become acrobats, as he dealt with his growing delight with Sarah's attention, the realization that it must soon end, the energy required to constantly construct scenarios for his affair and the nagging guilt, itself constantly re-stimulated by Dawn's smiling, trusting face. Still, he found himself anticipating Sarah's arrival at rehearsals, hoping to spend at least a few minutes afterwards together.

"Mr. Mack, I could make an announcement?"

The five pairs of ears in the sanctuary all turned to hear who wanted to announce what.

"What about?"

Sarah leaned in close, as if sharing a secret, and squeezed his hand.

"'Bout my wed'n."

The straight-laced Mack enjoyed what he was certain was a joke, and they winked at each other as she joined the small group of women quietly gossiping in the choir pews. Mack waited a few more minutes, until there were enough men present for the rehearsal to begin, made his weekly speech about starting on time, and began to run through Sunday's hymns. Half hour later, when they took a break, he invited Sarah Benjamin to make her announcement.

"Thank you Bulla Mack. Well, I really don't know how ta say this. I know some'a y'all probably see me with a light-skin young fella… a really boss young man? Well…y'see…he..we…we get'n married next October. We get engaged last night."

Somewhere amid the shrieks and shouts, John Mackenzie was hit with a sledge-hammer---up side his head, so to speak. While the members of the choir crowded around to congratulate Sarah and to get a look at the ring, Mack begged to be excused, coughed loudly and rushed to the nearest washroom, where, seated on the white, fiberglass throne, he cried.

"How you could do that? I thought we was more than that, I mean, not even a word."

"Sorry if you didn't take me serious when I try to tell yuh. But I tell you from day one, this a temporary thing."
"This the fella wth the red sports car?"

Sarah's surprise was clear. Until that moment, she had controlled the tone and direction of the conversation, and enjoyed having Mack off balance.

"When you see him?"
"I…er… I see him ..through the corner to the mechanic."
"When?"
"I dunno."
"Don't lie to me!"
"When you drop him there."
"You mean ta tell me you does follow me around? Well, I'll be damn."
"Not followin' you around, really. Just one day, I …"

Sarah left. She was furious. Mack sat in the restaurant, looking at the spot where she had been. That was the end of that. The sudden hunger he felt would be the final morsel in this feast of emotional upheaval, and he would finally get on with his life.

Over the next month Mack's life did in fact return to normal. Sarah returned to her former distance, as they seldom spoke, and then only formally. Her wedding date was still many months away, but her fiancé now occasionally visited Friendliness Baptist. But Mack's jealousy was difficult to conceal, and he missed Sarah's openness.

The first rainy season in the Bahamas begins in May and lasts through June. Especially early in the season the showers are short, and relatively light, and most Bahamians wait them out in conversation under cover. On this particular night it was raining lightly as the rehearsal ended. Most of the choir left before a heavier shower began, but Mack, Sarah and two other ladies had remained to polish a trio selection for the next Sunday's service. When they had finished, the other two ladies shared an umbrella to their cars and Sarah headed for the office to use the telephone, leaving Mack to collect the hymnals. As he stacked the last handful on the shelf, Sarah emerged from the office, a concerned look on her face.

"'Whats the matter. Sister B?"
"Elvis was supposed to come back fuh me, but he's not here, an' I can't reach him at home. An' jitneys don't run this late."
" I could drop you home, y'know."

The windshield wipers clicked away, giving the silence a rhythm, as Mack and Sarah stared into the downpour. Halfway to her house, Sarah spoke for the first time.

"Bulla Mack. Is somethin' I bin want'n to say. I shouldn't'a walk out like that. Sorry."
"No. You were right. I didn't have no business followin' you around. That was wrong, an' you were right."

Neither Mack nor Sarah noticed that the car, as if on its own power, had turned towards the waterfront, as they apologized to each other as if the words were clean, fresh water, and they had just crossed the desert. But soon they were seated on the shoreline, staring out to sea, listening to the music on the radio.

"I miss you, Sarah."

Without ceremony she moved over and kissed him. A moment later Mack had rediscovered his obsession, and they had agreed to meet again the following evening. Neither of them seemed anxious to talk about her impending marriage, or about anything else, for that matter.

CHAPTER SIX

Mack was nervous. As the fat, white lady searched for the correct key to the apartment, he looked around to see if there was anyone around who might recognize him. As soon as the door opened, he hustled inside and closed it behind him.

"You see, we would like to have someplace tuh put up people who come in from time to time. You know what I mean?"

The lady smiled to herself, having heard every reason in the book for renting an apartment on Paradise Island, to be used only 'from time to time'. She watched him in private amusement as he checked the curtains, the air-conditioning and the bathroom, ignoring the kitchen and the porch. Moments later he had paid two month's rent, and was on his way back to work, hoping Dawn Emily had not called.

But his wife had noticed the changes in his behavior. He had taken up early-morning walking, joined a gym and switched from boxer shorts to briefs. On the other hand, their sex life had gradually improved, as Mack had gotten more adventurous. When she mentioned the changes to her friend Emily Percentie, they agreed it was probably a late reaction to passing the age of forty. Mack was simply feeling his age.

Later that same day, Mack left his office again, this time for a routine visit to Customs Warehouse, where he had to inspect items which had arrived with a Duty-free status for some client or other. This time, however, he took a detour. The spotlessly-clean, red sports car was parked beneath one of the countless black olive trees arranged in military rows over the large parking lots, away from the small complex of neat, commercial buildings, sharing the shade with numerous vehicles. Making certain of his target, Mack re-read the license disc on the windshield. ELVIS BETHEL,

NORTH AVENUE. He looked around briefly, then knelt between the cars and drove the large ice-pick mercilessly into each of the four expensive, European tires. As he walked back to his own car, he whistled an old Boys Brigade tune, "We have an anchor". What he had done was wrong, but it was necessary.

It would be two or three hours before Elvis would stare at his tires in disbelief. Or read the type-written note under the windshield wiper, "CANCEL THE WEDDING". In his own mind, he would add, "OR ELSE".

Meanwhile Mack had returned once again to his office, where he would spend the rest of the afternoon staring out of the window in disbelief. It was the reason for his actions that terrified him. Sarah Benjamin had become the single focus of his attention, making his work difficult, his Church life strained, and his personal life confusing. Having always been proud of his ability to make decisions, he was suddenly finding them impossible. His days would begin with the commitment not to see her again, but by noon he had rationalized another meeting. Then some fictitious meeting or obligation would provide an opportunity for a trip or to some dark restaurant.

"Mr Mack, next year I'll be thirty. What you think I lookin' for? You cyan' gi' me what I want. You tied down. Like I tell yuh b'fore, this only for a time…til you get tired, or till Miss Mack find out."

His eyes burned as he stared across the dark, smoky space. The four or five bodies at the bar, bathed in flickering electronic light, sat immobile, transfixed by the courtroom drama radiating from the small square tube up near the ceiling, behind the bar. Like the other bodies in the booths and at the small, square tables, they were there not to be noticed, not be recognized, and out of courtesy to his regular customers, the owner never did. That was certainly why Mack was there, the third time in a week. Again, he promised himself that this would be the last time he would see Sarah…at least this way.

"You sure you goin' through with this marriage thing?"
"Yes."

He swallowed deeply.

"Then I gatta give up. I cyan keep this up."
"Thas up ta you."
"I mean...I like you...I like you a lot...but..."
"'Scuse me."

Without acknowledging his pain, Sarah rose and walked away, across the room, past the bar and through a doorway near the silent jukebox with the neon sign above marked "WASHROOMS", leaving a teary-eyed Mack counting the ways in which she had touched his life. Now, she must be gone. As she emerged a few minutes later, he saw her angelic face, as if in its own halo. God! She was so beautiful. How could he have not seen her before? And having discovered her, how could he give her up?

Suddenly, as if in another television movie, the room was transformed from a private meeting-place to a scream-filled Western tavern, as three figures burst into the room waving weapons. Mack heard the thunderous roar at the same time as he heard the wall nearby burst. As he ducked down behind the table, he could hear only one scream, seemingly drowning out the rest. Bottles smashed, chairs fell over, and men swore loudly as they scrambled for cover. But Sarah's scream rose above it all. Mack began to crawl across the dark floor, Marine-style, avoiding outstretched legs, broken glass and overturned furniture. But his return to reality was sudden.

"Where the hell you think you goin'?"

The bore of the shot-gun was inches from his head, and he could see the nervous finger curled around the trigger, squeezing the chrome appendage menacingly. He shut his eyes and waited for the explosion. Two seconds later the looked up, relieved, but more afraid than he had ever been.

"Allright, allright, I ain' goin' nowhere. Take it easy."
"I gat a good mind blow your ass away. You wan' be hero, eh?...Huh?"

All three were young men in their twenties, well dressed and well armed. Apart from the shotgun he was facing, there were two other guns. One reminded him of the gun he had begged his mother for when he was a boy-

--a Colt 45 Repeater--- the type he made sure his own children never had. Having never seen a real gun up close, of course, he would not have known that this huge version of his childhood toy was called a .357 Magnum. The other gun looked more like a toy. It was black, appeared to be made of plastic, like something he'd seen advertised last Christmas as an "Astro-Blaster". Mack would later learn that the Israeli Uzi was the most serious of the weapons of terror.

The young man threatening Mack's life was tall---very tall---and thin. His shrill voice seemed to come from a long way away, reinforced by a loud speaker.

"Now, y'all shut y'ass. An' empty the register. NOW."

He was now talking to the cashier, a rotund black girl, trying desperately to hide behind herself. On his silent command, the young man with the Magnum shoved a plastic shopping bag into her hand, and pointed the gun at her head. She did not hesitate to comply.

For a moment, Mack almost forgot the source of his predicament. But now the shortest, fattest young man with a pot-marked face had grabbed her by the hair and was twisting her neck mercilessly. Her eyes rolled over with each jerk of her head, and her breasts, always a strain for her blouse, had burst free, and were jiggling freely. No-one but Mack noticed the breasts.

The confusion ceased as suddenly as it had begun, with the roar of the Magnum. Everybody stopped breathing.

"All right. Nobody move, nobody get hurt."

The young man had fired his gun into the ceiling, and walked with his full shopping bag to the door. He opened the door, motioned to his confederates to leave. As the short, fat felon inched towards the door, he dragged Sarah with him, keeping her between him and the darkened room. Mack started to rise, but the cold steel of the shotgun butt met his forehead and sent him sprawling back onto the floor. By the time he could clear his head and rush towards the door with several of the other patrons, the sound of fire-crackers and breaking glass sent him diving to the floor for cover again. The glass windows and door to the small club were riddled by machine gun fire from the parking lot. A few seconds later they were gone, taking Sarah with them, leaving only the sound of screeching tyres, cursing patrons and a terrified John Mackenzie.

CHAPTER SEVEN

"Hey, you cyan' go. You gatta wait 'till the P'lice reach."
"Man, I gatta call my wife, an' this phone ain' workin'."

As Mack's eyes pleaded with the other victims for sympathy, for permission to return to his event-less life, they found the silent condemnation which he had hoped to avoid. Although none said it, he knew they had all known Sarah was there with him, and that she was not his wife.

"Anybody know who tha' gal is? I just hope they don't mess her up."

The lump on Mack's forehead was the same size as the one in this throat. Without speaking he got up again and walked into the washroom to try to vomit that lump away. He washed his face and returned, a bit more composed.

"The lady's name is Sarah Benjamin. She ain' gat no 'phone at home so I guh haveta go tell somebody. But first, I wan' go look around, see if I see her. Them boys look like they on somethin', an' I don't trust them. Tell the P'lice I comin' down to the Station later."

Once in his car, his composure slipped again. What would he tell Dawn? What if they hurt Sarah? As he sped along the darkened streets, not knowing what he was looking for, the tears flowed down his face. But soon, he was in his own driveway, watching the kitchen lights come on. Dawn was waiting up for him.

"Dear, you would never believe what happen. After our meet'n at the Church this evening. Sister Benjamin ask me to help her with a li'l problem. You know she get'n married, right? Well, thas it. Her an' her boyfriend…fiancé…well, they having' some problems, an' she was just lookin' fuh someone to talk to. Now, you know me. I cyan' see no one with trouble an' walk away. An' she was cryin.' I figger it would take no more than half hour."

Dawn hugged him in relief and admiration. Her husband had a reputation for compassion. Certainly he had to talk to the child, even if it meant taking her to a dark, unsavory place like the Black Bottom. Of course, he could have brought her home, but in the final analysis, she conceded, the distraught child probably needed to be someplace where she felt comfortable. As Mack breathed a sigh of relief, he hoped he would find Sarah in time to have her corroborate his story. A minute later, he was on his way to the Police Station, hoping they had word on the young men. No luck. There had been three armed robberies that night, all involving three armed young men. The Black Bottom was the last, and although they had set up roadblocks island-wide, there had been no sign of them. Or of their hostage.

Sarah's sister Freda did not mince words.

"Is your fault. I tell her not to fool with you. You's a married man. You only trouble. If anything happen ta my sister, you guh pay. Is your fault an' you guh pay."

Her younger brother Cedric arrived as Mack was leaving, and Freda told him of his sister's predicament. Without waiting for details, he left to go help the Police search. Mack drove around aimlessly for an hour, arriving finally at a spot where he and Sarah often had brown bag lunches, where he said a long, silent prayer. Then he went home and went to bed. He did not sleep.

The telephone rang at six fifteen. The Police had found Sarah's body on the eastern end of the island. Without a word to Dawn, Mack walked quietly into the bathroom, locked the door and vomited again. Then he sat down and cried for almost an hour. Dawn, awakened by the telephone, guessed what had happened, and felt sorry for her overly sensitive husband.

CHAPTER EIGHT

The tall, skinny one was named Walter, after his grand-father, he was told. The short, fat one with the pot-marked face was Ed, short for Ednol. The average-looking young man with the bigger-than-average .357 Magnum was Tommy, as in Thompson. The three had already boarded the white, 32 foot Bertram, moored at the exclusive marina near the eastern end of the island, and were counting the results of a very busy evening. Of the three robberies, the Black Bottom had been the least lucrative, and the only one that got out of hand. It was, in fact, the first time that anyone had gotten hurt in the seven trips they had made.

As the speedy pleasure craft sped towards the northern end of Eleuthera, the three friends were more quiet than usual.

"We're in trouble."

Walter, driving the boat, agreed.

"What you wan' do?"
"I think we better get the hell out of here."
"Hey, hey. Ease up man. We ain' gatta go noplace."

Tommy had already divided up the money and secured three metal cash boxes in the secret compartment. The talk of running away made him uneasy.

"Hey, listen. Ain' nobody guh look for us in 'Briland, even if they get anything to go on. We ain' left no prints, the car wasn't ours, an' we just three fellas out fishenin' for the night. Man, head up the bluff, le's catch a couple'a yaller-tail or sumethin'."

They all laughed nervously. Half hour later they had passed under the bridge and followed the shoreline to a spot where small boys knew they could always catch something. The cold beer and the frozen bait were shared, and they fished until dawn. Ed and Walter were still worried, but Tommy's rationale was perfect. Besides, Corporal Beckles would warn them if there was a need to run.

Detective Corporal Norwood Beckles was Tommy's adopted brother, a CID investigator. They had both enlisted together, but Tommy had been discharged shortly after basic training for possession of drugs. Two years later, Beckles had transferred to CID, and made a name for himself. A year ago, a drug deal involving his brother had gone sour and Beckles had destroyed the evidence of his brother's involvement. The contract had been created. Since then he had had to use his position twice to protect his brother.

Meanwhile, the Police in Nassau had checked the records of the major marinas and airports. But they had ignored the smaller, privately-owned facilities. After all, they were all owned by fine, upstanding well-to-do citizens.

CHAPTER NINE

Sarah's funeral was held a week later, on the Sunday afternoon. The Church was packed. The first four pews n the middle were reserved for the immediate family, and were decorated with large, purple bows and white chrysanthemums. Special ushers, young ladies dressed in purple and white, had been provided by the Funeral Home, who had also arranged for two large, rectangular displays of wreaths, each completely filled with colorful tributes to a fine young woman. The pulpit was decorated with a large heart of red roses. The casket, chosen by Freda, was a soft, pink velvet, lined with white satin, with a framed print of Jesus in the Garden of Gethsemane in the open lid. Sarah herself would have been proud of her corpse, bedecked in a white silk blouse with ruffles at the neck and her Lodge regalia laid neatly between her breasts. Those perfect breasts.

Behind the family pews, row after row of uniformed Lodge women rocked from side to side in time with the organ, like music notes in a Disney cartoon, roly-poly bass notes and tall, thin treble notes, all moving in concert. From their vantage points on the platform, the choir members watched the colorful parade through tear filled eyes, each ashamed of how little they knew about Sarah Benjamin, the alto.

Freda sobbed quietly onto Elvis Bethel's chest. She listened intently to the words of the hymns she had sung so many times, but which were suddenly so poignant, so perfect for the moment. The tears flowed freely as the hair on her neck stood up at the end of the first verse of the second hymn. "The Lord's My Shepherd." She listened to the consoling words of Reverend Percentie, seemingly assuring her that Sarah was now with the Lord, as if he knew for certain. She listened to "The Holy City", the special selection by the choir in her sister's honor. But bubbling beneath her sorrow, like guavas boiling for the duff, was an anger she could not contain, an anger which finally boiled over when Cedric went forward to read the obituary.

"The Lord is my strength and my salvation. I come to Him in prayer and supplication, knowing that I am unworthy."

Cedric, soft, deliberate speaking style had been perfected while working as a DJ in a number of night-clubs, before he started his small K-9 security business.

"When I was a child, I spake as a child. I acted as a child. When I became a man I put off childish things."

His black shark-skin suit was perfectly pressed. His white cotton shirt and striped, black-and-white tie made him look like a magazine ad. But his face exposed his pain.

"My sister Sarah is GONE."
"Amen."
"She is in the Lord's hand."
"Amen."
"They say only the good die young."
"Amen."
"But my sister did not die in hospital. She had no disease, no cancer. She didn't drown or have a car accident. No. She was taken away from us by animals, who took her for nothing more than a piece of thing, that they could use and then throw away. Un-Godly young men, who prey on the defenseless."

The congregation had gone stone silent. This was not the usual obituary, and Reverend Percentie was shifting in his tall, leather throne, Cedric continued, as if possessed.

"My sister Sarah is GONE. But it ain' right. And I pray forgiveness for the thoughts in my mind…"

That was when Freda's voice exploded n the sanctuary.

"An' I pray forgiveness for that hypocritical choir-master, who was there with my sister for nut'n else but to seek after the flesh. Them boys might'a kill Sarah, but she wouldn't a never been there if it wasn't for him."

The silence hung for what seemed like an eternity, broken finally by a lone female voice from the rear of the Church.

"Amen. I KNOW sup'm was goin' on."

Brother Mack jumped to his feet, stared down at Freda's fiery eyes for a moment, then walked quickly towards the Choir room, passing close to a stunned Cedric at the podium. With tears flowing down his cheeks, he removed his robe and staggered outside. Dawn Emily was standing near the door.

"What she talkin' 'bout Mack?"

The answer was all over his face, smeared with the tears. Without another word, she turned and walked away, past the small crowd gathering outside the side door, past the parking lot filled with shiny cars, past the huge, black hearse, and out onto the street, Mack stood on the top step, paralyzed, until she was out of sight, around the corner. Suddenly, he knew he had to follow her. Or his life would never return to normal. He remembered anxiously trying to get his key into the car door. Then the lights went out.

When they came on, there was something in his nose, but he couldn't raise his hand to remove it. He was trying to open his eyes, but all he saw was a fuzzy whiteness. His head seemed to weigh a ton, each ounce the bearer of a pound of pain. He closed his eyes again, and listened. There were voices near-by, one male and two female, talking quietly, as if in the presence of the dead. He tried again to open his eye, only to find a large, female face inches away from his, still out of focus. A few seconds later he was completely awake. Reverend Percentie explained how Cedric had left the podium and gone straight to his car to get a base-ball bat, walked up behind Mack in the parking lot and slugged him. If the small crowd had not been watching him from the side entrance, he might have killed Mack. He had been out for almost seven hours, and it was now near midnight.

Emily Percentie had not seen or heard from Dawn. After the Funeral she had gone immediately to the house, where Phillipa was at home alone, reading. No, she had not seen or heard from her mother, and they began their own search. Emily assured her that her father would be fine. Phillipa knew her mother well, how sheltered she had been, how dependent upon the stability she and Mack had built, and she could not imagine her on the streets of Nassau so long after dark.

But Dawn was more resourceful then they all imagined. She needed time to think, so she had used her credit cards and checked into a small hotel, where she stayed for the next five days. There she wrote letter after letter to her husband, none of which would be mailed. When Mack was released, he joined in the search.

Late Wednesday nigh, after sealing yet another twelve-page letter which she promised this time to mail, she went for a walk around the hotel gardens. The newspaper in the wastebasket had her face on it.

Phillipa was overjoyed to hear her voice. Mack was dying to see her, speak to her. But she had no intention of seeing him, or of returning to the house while he was there. She announced that she would find an apartment, refusing to even speak to her penitent husband on the telephone.

Their friends tried their best to coax her back home, but she had been hurt badly, and her prayers and meditation seemed to be leading her to a separation. Her marriage was a sham. Her husband had betrayed her trust, destroyed the palace of wonderful, shared thoughts, dreams and experiences which they had spent twenty six years building. At forty-eight, it would be difficult to start again, first to clean out the festering wound, removing the stench of Mack's unfaithfulness, then beginning the long and difficult process of creating a new trust, a trust which would always be vulnerable to the memory of this moment. And she was so tired.

On Thursday night, Mack did not sleep. He found himself parked outside Dawn's hotel just before sunrise Friday, fingering a short note.

DEAR DAWN,
I HOPE YOU AND GOD BOTH FORIVE ME. THE HOUSE IS MORE YOURS THAN ITS MINE. I DON'T NEED A HOUSE WITHOUT YOU. WHAT I DID WAS BAD. AND I HAVE NO EXCUSE. YOU ARE A GOOD, GOD-FEARING PERSON AND THE BEST WIFE AND MOTHER IN THE WORLD. GOD BLESS YOU. GOOD BYE. I'LL ALWAYS LOVE YOU.

MACK"

He got the Night Manager to place the plain white envelope marked MRS D MACKENZIE into the designated letter-box and drove to the airport. His relatives in Freeport owned apartments, and his export-import firm had a branch office there. There he could tread water while figuring out what to do with his rapidly –crumbling life.

His family had been shattered by his indiscretion---his one unfaithful episode in twenty-six years ---a romantic liaison which had begun with a simple question and exploded into an insanity which left his mistress dead, as if by his hand. His children had all voiced their disappointment in him and their support for their mother. His coworkers were shocked, some suggesting that early retirement might be a good idea, at half the pension he expected. Reverend Percentie had offered his support, but it was clear he could not return to Friendliness Baptist Church after the funeral incident. And both Cedric and Elvis had publicly threatened his life. John Mackenzie needed to be somewhere else.

Having checked in for the early flight, he watched the crowd in the waiting area, curious that so many people would travel so early in the morning.

"This is the first boarding call for Flight Number 602 to North Eleuthera, now boarding Gate M…"

Mack saw several people rise mechanically and walk towards the glass doors leading to the ramps. On the queue there were a number of people Mack thought he recognized, but no names came to mind. The tall young man might have been the son of one of his school friends. He returned to his own reading. Fifteen minutes later, Mack was boarding his own flight, and was soon headed for Freeport, the so-called Second City.

Freeport had rescued thousands of Bahamians in the 60's when its booming economy had erupted in the pine forest of Grand Bahama, bringing a thriving resort and an industrial complex into instant existence. Now Mack hoped it would rescue him. Once seated, he closed his eyes and prayed for guidance. At seventeen thousand feet, he remembered the bore of the shotgun, the voice from far away, and the tall, thin young man.

"Oh my God."

The minute the airplane landed, Mack darted to the Police Station where he was introduced to Deputy Inspector Fellows, a huge man with a slight West Indian accent, a career officer who had come to the Bahamas on contract during the 50's and remained for several terms. He had applied for, and gotten citizenship immediately after Independence. Unfortunately after supporting the Opposition in a General Election, he found himself posted in Grand Bahama, his ascendancy curtailed forever. He listened to Mack, making notes on his standard-issue lined pad, with his standard-issue yellow pencil, and grunted acknowledgments. His response surprised Mack.

"If you are certain de fellow you saw was de one who rob de club an' kill de woman, I will inform Nassau, but I wouldn't expect much. You have no name, you only know he was on a 'plane to North Eleuthera, and you have a description which fits half the young men in de country dese days. Central will write up my report and decide that manpower don't allow such investigation. If it was me, I would go to North Eleuthera myself, an' try an' pick up de trail."

Mack stared at him in total disbelief, which turned to surprise when the Deputy Inspector added,

"I would take me a gun, an' if I see him I would place my gun to his head, make him tell me where the other boys are before I call de Police again. In fact, I would shoot the sons-a-bitches right there, get back on de plane an' carry on with my life. Dat would be justice. You cyan' go about killin' people an' expect to live like is nothin' happen."

He was serious. But it was not the proper advice. Two wrongs don't make a right, his mother used to say. If that was the attitude of the Police, what could he do? He decided to speak to his cousin Nehemiah, with whom he was to spend his recovery time.

His cousin, already late for an appointment at the other end of the island, did not mince words. He agreed with Deputy Inspector Fellows, adding that in any case Mack should have a gun for his own protection, since it was obvious that the young men could kill without concern. In fact, he practically forced him to take his small .38 revolver, which he said he had bought when the drug dealers started landing their airplane on the long, empty road he took each day to West End. It had never been fired, and he admitted that it would probably not be very helpful against the fancy semi-automatic weapons he saw on TV. But something was better than nothing.

Sometime in the seventeenth century a group of Englishmen calling themselves the Company of Eleutherian Adventurers thought they would settle a small Bahamian Island, which they called Eleuthera. They didn't last very long, as they found the island "barren, not fit for habitation." The soil was thin, where there was soil, and the land rocky and flat. And there was no shade. That was the North Eleuthera at which Mack landed in the BAC 1-11.

"Taxi, sir?"
"Yeah. Take me to town."
"Where you wan' go? North or south?"

He did not know.

Until half an hour ago Mack thought Eleuthera was a town or settlement. Although he had heard of Bannerman Town, Upper and Lower Bogue and Gregory Town, he had never connected those names with any geographic location. The driver also explained that, from a nearby pier, the Ferry could take Mack to Spanish Wells or Harbour Island, all part of what was known as North Eleuthera.

He thought it would be a good idea to stay at a small hotel in Gregory Town, and perhaps to rent a car, if he wanted to be free to explore the island. It was Saturday, and rental cars would be difficult to find, but Fats, as he called himself, always knew where to finds things. Later, he also suggested a place for lunch, a waterfront shed just north of Gregory Town called the Edge of Night Restaurant, where they chatted like old friends. Fats had met the flight the previous morning, and swore that there were only two strangers aboard, a Police officer, in to investigate a recent traffic fatality near the Glass Window Bridge, and the new school teacher for Spanish Wells. The teacher was a woman, and the Officer was tall, but not that thin.

The thought that a Policeman might be involved in robberies and in Sarah's death made the hair on Mack's neck stand up, and he remembered Deputy Inspector Fellows. Fats pointed the way, and Mack headed for Lower Bogue, the accident victim's home settlement. As he watched the old rented Toyota disappear northward, Fats amused himself that Mack's search must be woman-related. Why else would he be so determined?

Two hours later, he was awakened by the Toyota's engine next to his taxi-cab. Mack had embarrassed himself by almost confronting the Policeman in error. He was at a dead-end.

"Yuh know, suh. The only person who come in on tha' flight who was tall an' young was one'a them "Brilan' boys. One'a them fellas what does wear plenty gold."
"Wha's a 'Brilan' boy?"

Fats laughed aloud. Mack, embarrassed that he obviously didn't know something he should know, joined in the laughter, which Fats enjoyed even more.

"Thas them boys from "Ar Briland. They's usually travel in a pack, but one'a them was on the 'plane by he-se'f yesterday. Thas who I b'lieve you lookin for."

It took Mack a second or two to recognize the name of the small resort settlement. Harbour Island. Fats gave him directions to the ferry and twenty minutes later he was headed for Harbour Island. He would return to the mainland on the last ferry, which the Captain explained would leave promptly at six o' clock.

But Harbour Island was like almost any other settlement on the Family Islands. Most of the people in the settlement were related, and a stranger in town in search of a 'Brilander could mean trouble, so Mack found his questions met with blank stares, and he soon realized that as a stranger, he would not be allowed into their confidence. But he thought he might have seen a way to make contact with the 'Briland community.

At eight o'clock the following morning. Mack again boarded the ferry to Harbour Island. He was going to Church. Until he came across the tiny Baptist Church in Harbour Island, he had not thought about his choir at Friendliness Baptist for several days. The organist had been practicing alone, to the delight of the neighbors. Despite his disastrous liaison with Sarah Benjamin, he still considered himself a Christian, and was overjoyed to find a place to worship, especially somewhere where his story had not, as yet, been told. The Baptist community would be warmer, he thought, than the 'Briland community.

Mack had met the Pastor at several Conferences in Nassau, although he had never actually like him enough to be friendly. But today Mack would be very friendly. He greeted Reverend Smith warmly, and agreed to have Sunday dinner with his family after Church. During the service, which was like the re-birth offered to a fallen Crusader by the Holy Grail, he bathed in the redemptive spirit. By the time the lively choir sang the Doxology, Sarah Benjamin, the three young men, even Dawn Emily and the children, were bite-sized problems which he would attack again in the morning, with renewed vigor. For today, he would revel in his own salvation, and allow himself the luxury of the memories associated with Sunday dinner.

For Mack, who had been raised a Methodist, but switched denominations when he joined the Boys' Brigade, a typical Sunday began with Sunday School, followed immediately by the Morning Service, a dash home to listen to the weekly Catholic Hour radio show, where the stories of Saints and Converts would reinforce the recent sermon. Then there would be a hearty family meal, sumptuous spread of peas and rice, macaroni and cheese, potato salad and chicken or some of kind of pork or beef, washed down with Kool-aid or 'switcher'. Before there was time for the food to settle, it was back to Church for Baptist Training Union, and finally the Evening Service. The day ended with a Bible study session, then bed. But of all the activities of the day, it was the meal that provided the memories.

"That was a wonderful service, Rev, an' you gat a great choir."
Reverend Smith thanked him, introduced him to his wife Emma, and they headed for the house. As the men sat to chat and Emma served the food, Reverend Smith apologized for the music coming from a nearby room. His son had not been to Church, because he had not been feeling well. Perhaps he was now feeling better. A minute later Mack stared at the young man in the doorway in terrified disbelief.

His legs became numb, the only thing preventing him from turning and running away. In his mind, he reached for the .38 to protect himself, and began to sweat when he remembered that it was hidden deep in the bag he had left at the hotel. So Mack swallowed the lump in his throat, did his best to look the boy in the face, and bravely stretched out him trembling hand.

There was no indication as they shook hands or spoke that the young man recognized him, and Mack thought it was fortunate that the boy would not be joining them for the meal.

"What does you son do, Rev?"
"That boy? Bulla Mack, you don't know how I pray for tha' boy. Him an' tha' bunch a friends he gat. He does help 'roun' the marina sometimes, y'know? He's very good with boats, but he too lazy. He could'a bin a engineer or somethin' but he don't wan' leave them friends'a his."

He said no more about the youngsters until after the meal, when Rev and Emma invited him to sit for awhile on the porch. He was absorbed in the realization that he had an advantage on the three young men. While he remembered them, they did not remember him. Then Emma Smith asked him what brought him to Eleuthera. Lying was becoming easy.

"Oh, just a li'l time off. Maybe do some fishenin'."

"Hey, thas great, I gat a idea. Why don't you go out with Walter tomorra?"

No! There was no way he would place himself in that position---alone on the high seas with a known murderer. No way. But then, if the young man really did not recognize him, he could use the opportunity to force Walter Smith to tell him where the other boys were, using the revolver. God was surely making a way for him. So he accepted the invitation, even offering to pay for the boat. Reverend Smith would not hear of it.

That night, Mack prayed with a special fervor. He prayed for guidance. He prayed for strength. He prayed that he could get the boys together before they became suspicious. And after he nervously checked the chambers of the .38, he prayed for forgiveness.

CHAPTER TEN

The sun was just peeping over the horizon when the Bertram pulled up to the Government dock to pick up an anxious local tourist. But besides Walter, there was a crew of two - both the other bandits. Mack, wearing a large straw hat and shorts, hoped again that he would not be recognized. He appeared not to be.

Trying his best to appear at ease, Mack boarded the boat with his green-and-gold bag, the one bought by his wife Dawn Emily in Atlanta, the one he had taken to Freeport the night he first made love to Sarah Benjamin. "You need something for when you only goin' away for the day, or when we goin' picnickin'."

Inside were a towel, a spare shirt, his wallet, his Bible and the gun. The boat had brought everything needed for fishing, and soon he was seated at the stern, watching every move the three friends made, his bag never more than a few feet away. Quietly, among themselves, they whispered about his strange behavior, but they had all been promised a small bonus, and their customer could behave as strangely as he wished. He was going to have fun, or else.

As the Bertram sped towards the flats, the young men explained that the Boston Whaler being towed behind would be used to navigate the shallow waters, where some shoals reached only inches below the surface. That would be where they could catch Bone-fish, if they were lucky. They joked about people who had tried to eat Bone-fish without 'pulling' them, and found that the bones were so plentiful and disorganized that they could not eat the fish, while their skillful friends could eat heartily. No, Mack had never 'pulled' Bone-fish. Nor had he had the pleasure of catching them, although he had heard that they were among the best small game fish caught in the Bahamas.

"Here they come!"

A hundred yards away from the Boston Whaler the water seemed to be boiling violently. As the churning intensified, spread and came nearer, Mack could see flecks of silver in the water - millions of tiny flashes, watery reflections in the dawn light, like underwater Christmas lights.

"Look at them suckers."

The small boat was suddenly alive with activity, as Walter Smith and his two confederates hurriedly armed themselves and their passenger with shiny, lithe, fiberglass rods, all pre-set for bone-fishing. In a few seconds bait was set, lines cast, and Mack was fighting his first fish. By now, the boiling water was all around the boat. They could see the thousands of pure silver, eel-like fish, desperately darting to and fro, like shoppers at a going-out-of-business sale. For ten or fifteen minutes, the four men were soldiers in the same battle, landing fish after fish, as quickly as they could handle them. Then suddenly the fish were gone.

"Wha'...what hap'n?"

Walter jumped to his feet, straining his eyes towards the north of the Whaler. The crystal-clear water had suddenly revealed its mossy, coral bottom, a wonderful patchwork of pink and white brain coral, orange, white and black fan coral, mocha moss and a hundred other hues from nature's palette. Walter was searching for the reason for the sudden disappearance of the fish, as if he knew what the answer was, but not where it was. Finally, with an almost satisfied grin, he pointed towards a grey-and-white shadow the size of the boat, drifting slowly and silently near the shallow bottom, not more than twenty feet from them.

"Tiger shark!"

A chill ran up Mack's left side. He had never seen a real shark before except at the aquarium, but he was certain that this shark was circling the boat, the way they always did in the stories.

"Is it dangerous?"
"You jokin'? You wouldn't wan' meet one overboard."
"But I thought wasn't no dangerous sharks in the Bahamas."
"Thas a lie. Tiger, Bluefin, Mackeral an' Hammer-head. All'a them dangerous. Ain' guh be no more fish here dis mornin'. Le's go."

Tommie began collecting the rods, while Walter started the boat and Ed pulled up the anchor, all as if they had done this all their lives. But suddenly Ednol as overboard. He had leaned overboard to clear the anchor rope as Walter started to move, and lost his balance. Walter quickly turned the boat around, and he and Tommie leaned over the edge to pull their friend aboard.

"C'mon. Get in b'fore that thing turn. Shit! C'mon".

Until that moment, Mack had sat, paralyzed, watching this drama unfold, as if in an old movie. But then he saw his role in the spectacle. He casually pushed Walter and Tommie overboard, then began driving the boat away, back towards the Bertram.

While the boys yelled that this was not funny, screamed and cursed at the top of their lungs, he kept his face turned towards the Bertram, and sang one of his favorite hymns, "I Come To The Garden Alone", also at the top of his voice. Through the drone of the 45 horse-power outboard engine, and his own voice, he could hear the splashing as the young men swam after the boat, then the screams and a different kind of splashing, then the silence. He even imagined he saw the satisfied sharks smile as they left their breakfast-time feeding frenzy.

Once back on the Bertram, Mack took out his Bible and sat, facing back towards the now-peaceful flats, towards the perfectly-smooth, glistening water. It was as if the earth had been washed clean of a terrible pollution. He opened his Bible, leaned back and smiled, then raised his eyes to the sky.

"The Lord is my Shepherd, I shall not want. Yea though I walk through the valley and the shadow of death I shall fear no evil, for Thou art with me. Thy rod and Thy staff shall comfort me. Oh yeah. Thy rod and Thy staff..."

He laughed aloud, a long, hearty laugh, not at all in character for the conservative, carefully-controlled, boring Choirmaster that Sarah Benjamin knew. But then, none of this adventure involved that John Mackenzie. This John Mackenzie was celebrating the fact that the sea had done the Lord's work, with him as a witness. The evil-doers had perished at their own hands. They had fed on others in life, and their fate was to be fed to the sea. He smiled again, and continued reading his Bible aloud, rocking back and forth in the spring-loaded, game-fishing swivel chair.

The next afternoon, Air-Sea Rescue found him, still reading and singing in that chair. He would not, or could not, explain what had happened to the young men, or why supplies had not been touched, or where the uncleaned fish in the Boston Whaler came from, or why he had a gun in his hand bag. His answer to all of those questions was the same.

"Vengeance is Mine, sayeth the Lord. Amen."

Dawn Emily Mackenzie wept as she signed the admission papers. Neither she nor the doctors could understand the satisfied look on Mack's face as he sat, Bible-in-hand, on the small cot in the bare hospital room. Next to him was his old briefcase, full of salvaged sheet music, the only thing he had asked for when they brought him in. As his darkened eyes swept the room, he was pleased with his life. Dawn Emily was back, Sarah Benjamin's killers had been dealt with, and he had been instructed in a dream to start his own ministry, a one-man, musical ministry, without walls. This mental hospital would be a perfect place to find his first congregation.

EPILOGUE

The evidence of his years on the street clung to his body as he backed himself deep into the doorway, avoiding the wind and the direct view of the Policemen on their Bay Street beat. Tomorrow he would get an appointment to sing for the Governor, a boyhood friend of his, who once loved his music, but who now seemed too busy to appreciate the important things in life.

The two Police officers met on the corner, and both looked towards the waterfront. The beautiful baritone voice was unmistakable. They looked at each other as if to ask which one would investigate, then, as if on signal, turned and walked away, in the opposite direction. The Choirmaster was only celebrating Christmas.

Funeral services for the late Mr. John Mackenzie will be held at the graveside at Potters Field at 4PM on Thursday. Officiating will be the Right Reverend Dr. Otis Percentie of Friendliness Baptist Church. Mr. Mackenzie is survived by his wife, three children, and a number of other relatives.

www.ingramcontent.com/pod-product-compliance
Ingram Content Group UK Ltd.
Pitfield, Milton Keynes, MK11 3LW, UK
UKHW041959230426
12048UKWH00008B/421